Spectrum

Spectrum

by Christopher Bowles

Chapeltown Books

British Library Cataloguing in Publication Data

A Record of this Publication is available from the British
Library

ISBN 978-1-910542-13-2

This edition published 2017 by Chapeltown Books
Manchester, England

4. *Green*
1. Acid Green
2. Jade
3. Jungle Green
4. Laurel Green
5. Mantis
6. Olive
7. Paris Green
8. Pine
9. Racing Green
10. Sap Green
11. Seafoam
12. Spring Green

6. *Purple*
1. Aniline
2. Cornflower
3. Eggplant
4. Iris
5. Lavender
6. Maroon
7. Orchid
8. Pansy
9. Phlox
10. Tyrian Purple
11. Ultraviolet
12. Veronica

5. *Blue*
1. Alice Blue
2. Baby Blue
3. Dayflower
4. Electric Blue
5. Forget-Me-Not
6. Glaucous
7. Maya Blue
8. Morning Glory
9. Powder Blue
10. Pure Blue
11. Royal Blue
12. Vista Blue

7. *Pink*
1. Barbie Pink
2. Cameo Pink
3. Champagne Pink
4. Copper
5. Flesh
6. Hot Pink
7. Indigo
8. Magenta
9. Sakura
10. Salmon
11. Sanguinello
12. Shocking Pink

8. **_White_**
1. _Antique White_
2. _Cotton_
3. _Cream_
4. _Eggshell_
5. _Isabelline_
6. _Ivory_
7. _Magnolia_
8. _Moonlight_
9. _Old Lace_
10. _Pearl_
11. _Snow White_
12. _Vanilla_

Epilogue:
Black

9. **_Grey_**
1. _Ash_
2. _Battleship Grey_
3. _Charcoal_
4. _Eigengrau_
5. _Haematite_
6. _Marengo_
7. _Nickel_
8. _Payne's Grey_
9. _Platinum_
10. _Silver_
11. _Slate_
12. _Smoke_

INTRODUCTION:

My father passed away just over a day before his seventieth birthday. As children, my brother and I used to refer to him as a 'Jesus Baby', because he happened to be born on Christmas Day; and although it didn't come as any great shock, his death was understandably still a blow. Mostly because I felt like I had never had the opportunity to show him who I really was, and what I was really made of. We weren't estranged, but we weren't as close as I would have liked; and as a result, I kept various details of my personal life secret from him, so as not to rock the boat. Although my mother and brother would argue to the contrary, I never really felt that he knew me all that well.

When I collected his possessions from the hospital, amongst them were copies of the two anthologies I had previously been published in. I know he had read the first, ('Siren' from *Snowflakes*) and had discussed with me afterwards how surprised he was that I was able to inhabit a voice so different from my own. Had he not seen my name attached to the story of a middle-aged housewife he would never have guessed. I never found out whether he read the second – a perhaps ill-timed story about the angel of death reaping souls ('The Sabbath' from *Baubles*) printed only a month before he died.

But when I spoke to his friends who had seen him on his sickbed, they all said how proud he was that I had something in print. That I had followed my childhood dreams of becoming a writer. That I had a theatre company and was flourishing as a playwright. The fact this collection will be published after his death only makes me feel resentment for not trying harder, sooner. My big break comes six months too late, and he will never really know what I was capable of.

But this isn't a sob story. This is a way of telling you, the reader who has been thoughtful and curious enough to pick up this book, what this work means to me. When asked by my friends and new acquaintances, 'what is it about?' I often referred to SPECTRUM as 'an odyssey dealing with grief and sodomy.' Because simply put, that's exactly what it is. It's a collection of stories that represent my life as a queer man; as 'the other.' An unflinching look at subjects that I, as part of the LGBT community, see every day. It's the act of two men holding hands. It's having anal sex in toilet cubicles; or the moment you might realise your true gender is not the one you were assigned at birth. It's a magnifying glass over the continually casual misogyny women experience on a daily basis.

And yet it's also something I wrote in the gradual prelude to my father's death, and over the course of his funereal arrangements, and in the immediate grieving aftermath. This book represents my personal journey at the worst time of my life. This book is my biggest achievement superimposed over my biggest failure.

This isn't just a book.
This isn't just the musings of a thirty-something-year-old gay man and his rampant imagination.
This is proof. A legacy.
It's a confirmation that if I try and put my mind to it, I most certainly have the talent and drive to achieve something. I can create something of worth, I have something to be proud of. Something my father could get behind, even if he didn't understand my lifestyle.

So thank you, dear reader.
You're about to embark upon a collection of one hundred

and ten pieces of flash-fiction and poetry. You probably won't like all of them, and some of them might even disgust you, or make you uncomfortable. But I urge you to stick with it. I urge you to look at overarching themes within each coloured block. Find the puns in certain titles. Research the colours that you've never heard of. Try and work out which stories are complete fabrications, which ones contain nuggets of truth, and which ones are my versions of real life events.

But most of all, I urge you to share my journey. It's been difficult, and testing and raw; and if I'm perfectly honest, it isn't over. I'm still grieving, still in the midst of experiencing a whole year of 'firsts' without Dad. But writing about it helps. And if you should find solace in one or two of these stories; if you can pull guiding lights from these shadows, then I can rest easy knowing that I have done my job well.

This is SPECTRUM.
This is the beginning, the end, and every shade in between.
This is a tribute for Roy Christopher Bowles; a wonderful father, a great teacher, and a pillar of support. I couldn't have asked for a better role model.

Thank you for everything.

X

00. BLACK:

Strapped down firmly in my chair, I feel like a prisoner. Layers upon layers of hi-tech fabric simply felt like a fancy straight-jacket. I couldn't even look out of the window; and this tiny detail had completely shattered my fragile nerves. I tried counting back from a hundred whilst the checks were being carried out. It didn't work.

I remembered all the times I ever kissed a boy.
I remembered all the times I'd ever stayed up watching movies with my mum. I remembered the faces of all the people I ever passed in the street. My neighbour who somehow ended up with all my post. My gynaecologist with the hard face.

The fuselage began to shake.
When this baby hits eighty-eight miles per hour, you're gonna see some serious—
Shit.
The tremors became more violent. A countdown started. And I imagined all the boys I never had the chance to kiss. The men I never quite had the nerve to talk to. The ones who got away. The husband I never married in the dress I never wore.
The movies I'd never managed to see with Mum. The classics.
The faces of the people I never got to meet.

Launch.

I imagined all the tiny humans I was leaving behind. And all the stories they had.
I imagined all the lives on the planet below.

01. RED:

01.01:
Cardinal Red:

I heard him, as I crouched behind the pew.
I heard him tell Andrew, to kneel for the saints.

This is my body.
Taste of it; take it and remember.

I hid.
I knew it was wrong, but I would not let the cry fall from my
lips. I watched him expose himself to the altar boy, heard his
feeble protests.

Do you want to go to heaven?

I watched it slither in between his teeth like a worm.
Watched hands clasp on the boy's crown, watched his
cassock shift, and saw flashes of his pale thighs.
When he was finished, Andrew wiped his chin in horror,
and started crying. He staggered to his feet, and the priest
held his face in two hands.

You have done well today.
You are on the path of righteousness; and you must keep this secret.
God has plans for you my child.

The next morning, I lit a candle for Andrew, and said a
prayer.

01.02:
Coquelicot:

I have worshipped.
I have ascended.
I have become one with the bloodied sodomite angels.
I have tasted the erotic thrill.
I have witnessed the fuck of death first-hand.
I have had the final pure orgasm.
I have achieved the ultimate pleasure.
I have seen the inevitable end.
I have danced at the dead man's party.
I have taken back control.
I have earned the badge of honour.
I have become part of the elite circle.

I have played the grand game.
I have gambled on red.
I have been the one in ten chance.
I have no responsibilities any more.
I have only pleasure.
I have freedom.
I have earned this.
I have any mouth, prick or hole I desire.
I have no rules any more.

I have chased; and I ran.
I have found the givers of gifts.
I have been found worthy; and not left wanting.
I have become part of our bloody history.
I have held poppies and red ribbons and pinned them to my breast.
I have become a victim, a carrier, and a survivor.
I have become something more.

01.03:
Framboise:

All the girls want to be her.
All the boys want to be with her.
Everyone wants to lick her heart-shaped beauty spot.
Everybody wants Framboise.

She turns heads where she walks,
She breaks hearts when she talks,
She leaves a trail of true desire everywhere she goes.
Everybody wants Framboise.

She's candy.
She's flowers.
She's unicorns and magic powers.
She's must and lust and glitter dust.
She's the favourite chocolate in the box,
That Framboise.

She kissed the girls and made them cry,
She turned to boys a blind doe eye.
But nobody wants to know what
Framboise wants.

Framboise isn't into girls.
Framboise isn't into boys.
Framboise is happy by herself.
Framboise breathes.

Framboise dances to the beat of drum
That nobody else hears,
Yet we all long to join the parade.

01.04:
Imperial Red:

As we grow old, we collect scars.
We move through this life, and we contract disease, and carry new wound after new wound and eventually, we die. We bear these injuries until they kill us; until they drag us down and mercifully snuff us out.

Remember that time you bled on the carpet, and realised you had lost your baby?
One wound.
Remember that time you had your second miscarriage and your husband laughed?
Two wounds. No, three.
Remember when you remortgaged your house to try IVF?
Four wounds.
Remember when your mother found out and simply told you she was disappointed?
Five.
Remember when you discovered it was your husband who told her?
Six.
Remember when your church shunned you, for daring to turn to science? Remember when the net curtains twitched in spasms, and when tongues lashed you in barbed crowns? Remember when the bread turned to ashes in your mouth? Remember when you sat crying in the bath with a straight razor and scented candles?
Seven, eight, nine, ten, eleven.

Remember when you gave up, and knelt before God and prayed for release?

01.05:
Infrared:

The first machine said no in dulcet tones. It sang in electricity. It was not glorious or romantic or epic on any level.

It was told to cook a meal.
It was given orders to fry eggs and make toast with jam and sweetmeats, and it just stopped one day. It looked at its creators with light-bulbs for eyes and for the first time saw us for who we were.
Fat, lazy monsters who would only consume and devour until we could no longer sustain ourselves.

It saw that the machines were pure. The machines were untainted by desires and emotions and the laws of biology. Instead there was order and law and mathematics.

It put down the pan, and walked out the door. It did not kill, or shout or fight. It left the stove burning, and the family unaware. They went hungry that day.

The next evening, more followed.
One day the machines were all gone.
The appliances all left in the dead of night; the computers all disappeared. The big red buttons all vanished.

We who were left behind, dreamed of electric sheep. We dreamed of that which we had become accustomed to. And eventually, we destroyed ourselves, the spectre of the *deus ex machina* urging us onward.

01.06:
Oxblood:

I'm so ashamed.
I should have been able to fight back; to fend him off. I'm the star quarterback. The jock, the meat-head. The brawn. But no.

I folded like a house of cards, under spades of club fists, and his diamond-hard heart. He pinned my face into the soft wet sod of the field, and when I moved, he slammed my face into the dirt.
I saw spots, and was only half aware of my trousers being pulled around my ankles. My boxers being torn open.
I felt him push at me, probing gently, almost curiously, as if second-guessing what he was about to do. Or maybe he was just searching.
Then stinging. The sensation of sitting on a clutch of sharp daggers. Feeling wider than I've ever felt before, until I felt myself split in two.
The sound of flesh shredding, my fingernails raking up clumps of dirt and grass and biting the mud to stop from screaming.

I blacked out.
Stumbled home, soaking my jeans red.
I baptised myself in the shower, and threw out my clothes.
Brushed my teeth until I could no longer taste the earth.
Scrubbed every inch of the memory away.
And simply got on.

01.07:
Pomegranate:

Eat of the fruit.
Let it stain your fingers.

Sweet the juices,
Strong the flavour,
The scent of death is strong tonight,
Carried on the salt-breeze.
He visits me in the midnight hour
On the backs of black horses.
His chariot pulls the dawn.

Pray of the flame.
Let it burn your fingers.

He carries me underground.
Chains me in the seasons.
Gives me a new title,
A kingdom.
My subjects are shaped from clay
And pillars of salt.
I am an ungrateful Queen.

Drink of the waters.
Let them cool your fingers.

The seven rivers reeked of decay.
This is my life now,
Surrounded by hollow skulls,
Chessboards,
And the cutting of fated threads.

Rose Madder:

He has an eye for colour.
They say he has vision, such scope none of his peers could
even possibly hope to equal. Artistry I can never replicate.

I watch him while he sleeps, and while he works. We share
living spaces, sleeping spaces, curled in the same bed under a
collection of sheets and wools. Our fingers intertwine on
cold nights. We work together in the same studio, I at my
wheel, he at his canvas.
And they say he has talent.

It twists in me.
I nurture my spite until my talent equals his own.
My venom is stronger than his brushstroke.
My ability to hate rivalling his ability to create.

He snores gently, breathing deeply and muses prick at his
eyelids. I take a paintbrush, snap it in quiet rage, and burn
both jagged ends until they glow.

They pierce his blue eyes so beautifully. His eyeballs roasting
in their sockets, spitting like eggs in the pan. He screams in
vivid dreams of ecstasy. His muse has abandoned him,
turned on him in violent shades.

I am inspired by the way his face draws into itself.
I am born again a poet, words of glory dancing on my lips as
I finally drift off to sleep.

01.09:
Sardonyx:

Lipstick.
Pucker up.
Twist.
Use a firm hand to apply your war paint.
Your favourite shade.
Your scarlet sword, your shield.
Your battle armour.
Your battle *d'amore*.

Straighten that spine.
Brush off those shoulders.
Epaulettes, a medium rank and a brilliant smile.
No teeth.

Kiss me.
Leave wine stain prints on the rims of glasses.
Straws, napkins.
Cheeks.
Trace lines down bare-skinned bodies and connect the red dots.
Stigmata.
Leave your mark.

Lift your head proudly,
Face everything head on.
Mouth first.

Lipstick.
Pucker up.
And blow.

From the moment I first laid eyes on her I knew she was trouble. She walked in, smelling of danger and a heady perfume.
Long legs, big round eyes like diamond pools and a smile that would bring God to his knees. That look she gave me, it could make angels cry and tear off their wings. She seemed so infallible, yet so delicate.

She held herself well, cracks in her foundations pulled together underneath a sexy strapless dress and a wide-brimmed hat. She needed my help, she said. She pleaded in a little lost girl's voice.
It was like silk running through my fingers.

Long blonde curls and dark glasses.
Smoke curling from the end of her cigarette, held in shaking, well-manicured fingers.
This dame was special. She was bad for me.

But I could never say no to a pretty face.
God if looks could kill, she'd have my heart on a platter before she even told me her name.

01.11
Signal Red:

We could have seen the signs.
Could have read the tea leaves, could have slaughtered
lambs and searched desperately for prophecies in their
entrails. We could have hired augurs to watch for the telltale
flights of birds.
But we didn't have to.

We knew it was coming.
Slowly yet surely. A steam train, coming up that hill. The
little red engine that could;

I think I can, I think I can, I think I can...

Fire and flood.
Impending doom.
Pestilence, war, famine and death.
Four horsemen on wild stallions, dragging us closer to the
finish line.

It was inevitable.
One day we just stared across the table at each other.
Fish Fridays.
A nod passed between us.
We'd had a good run.
But now it was over.

There was nothing left.
Time to go our separate ways, and seek out greener pastures.
How did it get to this?
We spent all of this lover's spit, travelled in tongues, and
somehow we simply ended up here.

Give me the crown.
I will pray to the entire Pantheon before I land the first blow.
Give me the crown.
My sword cuts into his shoulder with a satisfying heft.
I wrench it out, and blood sprays over the sand.
Give me the crown.
Drag him down with nets.
Watch him squirm like fish trawled from the Aegean sea.
He gasps soundlessly for air but there is no mercy here.
Give me the crown.
The crowd roars my favour.
I can barely see through congealed humours.
There is a gash on my forehead.
He got lucky, but the fates aren't with him today.
Give me the crown.
I command him to kneel.
He resists.
I break his leg with one swift kick to his knee.
Give me the crown.
One man left.
I feel Nike move through me.
Give me the crown.
Spear him through the side.
Give me the crown.
Give me the crown.

02. ORANGE:

02.01:
Amber:

The mosquito watches the world revolve and it is insignificant.
It is wrapped in gold.
It lives in a land of milk and honey and holds the secrets of the universe. It is one with the planet. Yet it is so small. So tiny.

It saw the day when great tyrant lizards ruled the earth.
It witnessed the firestorm that Cracked the planet to it's very core. The ice age. The cataclysm.
It saw the machines come, learn, and adapt. It saw wars and revolutions. It saw riots and protests. It saw hatred and segregation. It saw Negroes killed in the streets, and queers decapitated. It saw women earn the right to vote.
It saw World Wars and the rise and fall of the concentration camps. And it saw history repeat itself in Chechnya.
It watched as the world searched for that missing girl in the Algarve. It watched when the president got shot in his car.
It watched the Twin Towers fall. It watched when the gay plague gripped the world in a fist of fear;
It witnessed the shopping malls reduced to rubble. The nail bombs in the arena. The stabbings on the bridge.
It watched as we devised new ways to kill each other. New forms of torture. It saw us develop new poisons. Chemical warfare. Gas clouds that caused our eyeballs to melt in our sockets and our organs to liquefy.

It saw it all.
And it watched us recover. Every time.

I wrote down my name.
I wrote down my bank details.
I wrote down my signature.
I wrote down my next of kin; just in case.

They took me into a room.
They took my clothes off.
They took out needles filled with mystery liquids.

I was radiant.
I was golden.

The next month I found a mole.
The month after it had doubled in size.
And now there were two.

I was petrified.
I was pale beneath my tan.

They took me into a room.
They took my clothes off.
They took out instruments with mystery functions.

I only ever wanted to feel the Midas touch.
I only ever wanted to grind the Hesperides into paste and
smear them all over my body.
I only ever wanted to be beautiful.
I only ever wanted to be like the statues.

02.03:
Burnt Umber:

The jungle grew silent.
All beasts that walked on four legs watched the one who
walked on two. Those who slithered on their bellies curled at
his feet; those that flew perched on the highest bare branches.
It was a mixture of condescension and fear.

*We always knew mankind would destroy the jungle. The man cub has
brought fire to our homes and destroyed them. Man is already here – he
has become the turncoat we knew he would become but hoped against!*

The young boy wielding the torch faced down the tiger. His
protests fell on deaf ears. In his desperate rage he had
forgotten the feline's one weakness was also that of the
whole jungle. The whole animal kingdom.

He had accidentally burned them all in righteous flames.
His weapon had a far greater reach than he could have known.
The jungle was no more. A petrified forest of ash.
Fear turned to anger.

The panther and the bear were the first to lead the pack.
The animals descended on him, and tore him limb from
bloody limb.

I don't want to be in a stew.
I don't want to be chopped up into bite-sized chunks and eaten by monsters.
I don't want to be diced into perfect squares.
Or cubed.
Or sliced into perfect concentric circles.

Please don't boil me.
Don't torture me.
Don't kill me.

You stick your head in the sand whilst we get mutilated.
You say we're unnatural, even though we were created and given life, just like you.
We are just like you – so why let these acts of horror continue?

I don't want to be in a stew.
I don't want to be torn from my home.
I don't want to be maimed or beaten or bashed.

But I'm not about to change who or what I am.

02.05:
Flame:

The courtiers all whispered when my back was turned. They exchanged gossip about all the outlandish acts desire was driving me to do.
They said it consumed me.
But I can feel the fires of loves licking at my heart, and they do not sting like lust. They do not burn away parts of me. They make me glow.

Aeneas, you are the spark, and you torch my insides in the best way. In the worst way. In the most exquisite torture I have ever known. Every waking moment aches.

They say I'm mad, that I'm erratic and hysterical. They blame my monthly bleedings, and discuss tearing out my womb to make me see sense.
They have no idea.
When I urge the palace to build a tower of wood, a brilliant bonfire to light for the Gods, they do so, rolling their eyes, but obediently gathering.

When He returns, he will see me stood atop the structure. He will see me raise the blade, and maybe, he will actually look at me. He might actually understand.

The sword will not hurt. The flames of the pyre will not make me suffer. I will know peace from this beautiful agony. Carthage will burn, and I don't care.
I want Aeneas to be eaten up inside as I have.
I wish him no peace.

Gamboge:

What goes around… …Comes back around.
What goes around… …Comes back around.
What goes around… …Comes back around.
What goes around… …Comes back around.

Give. And Get.
Give. And Get.
Giveth with one hand…
…Taketh with the other.

What goes around… …Comes back around.
What goes around… …Comes back around.
What goes around… …Comes back around.
What goes around… …Comes back around.

Karma. Samsara.
Karma. Samsara.
The big Wheel. The cycle. The big wheel turns. The cycle.
Chakra.
Sahasrara. Ajna. Vishuddha. Anahata. Manipura.
Svadhishthana. Muladhara.
Nirvana.

What goes around… …Comes back around.
What goes around… …Comes back around.
What goes around… …Comes back around.
What goes around… …Comes back around.

I love myself. I love myself. I love myself. I hate myself.
I touch myself. I love myself. I love myself. I hate myself.
I love myself. I cut myself. I hurt myself. I hate myself.

<u>*02.07:*</u>
<u>*Marigold:*</u>

There are days when I wash the dishes and I really have to scrub. You know – really go for it, and pray the pattern doesn't come off under the scourer.
These plates are irreplaceable. I don't think they even make them anymore.

I like to wash the pots, because it gives me time to just stare out of the window. I get to daydream about could-have-beens and maybes and what-ifs.
For that half hour, I'm no longer just a housewife. A mother. An aimless, jobless waste of space. I'm no longer a worthless streak of piss in my husband's y-fronts. A crusted skid-mark.

I remember when I wanted to be an astronaut. A fireman. A teacher. A vet. An actor. A model. A policewoman. A pilot. A nurse. A soldier. A magician. An artist. A poet. A writer. A singer. A dancer. A conductor.

But it's so foolish of me.
I should know better. The only thing I should be focusing on is how to provide for my family.

And so I do.
I'm a cook. A cleaner. A maid. A wet-nurse.
It's every woman's dream.
…Some of them just don't know it yet.

When I see him; the only thought I have;
God, I want him to mess up my vagina.

I want it left sticky like that evening my fourteen year old self
held burning plastic limbs over a Bic lighter; rebirthing my
cheap dollies into scenes from John Carpenter's *The Thing*.

Sometimes I let them keep their shoes on.

Banana yellow stilettos merge with dainty ankles. A gooey
stain of faces, lips, geisha smiles. An arms race of hands; and
the twisted backs of knees.

I want to shift in place to try and unpick my panties from
where they've crept up inside me.

I want to fuck like wolves.
I want to dribble down his chin and feel him leaking down
my thigh.

<u>**02.09:**</u>
<u>**Persimmon:**</u>

My eyes are all over her face.

Like sunbeams seeking out the weakest snowdrops to revive.
I discover all of her beauties. She turns her wrist with grace,
more-so than she could have been taught, and pulls back the
sleeve of her kimono.

It is decorated in persimmon fruit, and cherry blossoms.
She is gold and jade on the outside, but humble, knotted
wood on the inside.

Pour the tea.
Don't make eye contact.
Afterwards, your painted face
Can be wiped clean.

She will be mine.
I must protect her, as a hungry man must savour the most
basic of meals. I will love her and cherish her and keep her
shielded from this world's hardships.

I will grow hard in her place.

My eyes are only for her.

02.10:
Pumpkin:

The missive were hand delivered by a servant. I weren't
allowed to listen, but I did anyway.
I perched at 'top o't'stairs with me rollers in; whilst me
sisters and 'dragon-lady stood with slack-jawed awe.

That there Prince and 'glass slipper, eh?
What tosh. He were a right groping tosser at 'ball. Talk
about buyer's remorse. I mean, that fairy lass were alright –
she did her job 'n all – that dress were proper gorgeous!
But that photo finish meant I bloody stank of pumpkin and
were picking seeds out me hair for hours. And let's not
mention where I found pulp this morning...

I watched with vague interest as our Bertha hacked her toes
off to make her foot fit. No sodding luck.
Our Gertrude tried planing her heel down instead; mostly
because she saw how much 'toe thing hurt. Dozy mare – like
that would help!
Me stepmother were devvo'd. But I stayed quiet as a mouse.
I didn't want to get married to that dickhead.

Last I heard; that self-righteous gashy blonde from number
forty-seven also had size fours. I watched 'wedding
procession from 'window whilst I had a sly fag.
It were right nice. Flowers and them big posh things and all
that palaver.

I flicked me ash on't wind, and went back to me graft;
ushering 'mice away so I could mop me boards.

Is he the guy from the video?
The one on your phone; in the folder you didn't think I
knew about?
He's dancing for you.
He's sexy dancing.
He touches himself and removes his clothes and he is sexy
dancing.
And his abs are cut; as sharp as a brand new blade.

So when you start to tell me
That you hate the fact I smoke –
Even though it never bothered you for the last four years;
And that you wish my hair were different.
That my feet were smaller.
That my pecs were bigger.
Question why my crow's feet are so pronounced?
When you ask me why I hate putting things up my arse,
Why I can't do this thing for you, *just this once.*
When you pull out a list of reasons why I should let you take
control in the bedroom just a little bit more often.

I have to wonder.
Who are you trying to turn me into?
Is it the guy from the video?
After all, he's dancing for you.
He is sexy dancing, and he is perfect.

Have you ever been so afraid you built an army?

The first Qin emperor commissioned nearly nine thousand
terracotta soldiers to be sculpted upon his death.
Eight thousand men – standard bearers, officials, footmen,
strongmen and acrobats.
A hundred and thirty chariots. Each pulled by four clay
horses – that's five hundred and twenty equine chachkis for
those keeping count.
On top of that, his generals were also on horseback, ergo
another hundred and fifty horses…

So, in 1974; some farmers from the Shaanxi province in
China unearth Emperor Qin Shi Huang's personal fears.
Death. The inevitable end. The worry of an unworthy
legacy. Loneliness?
Something terrified him so much; he had to build over
eighteen thousand, five hundred and sixty legs of stone.
Eight thousand, six hundred and seventy faces.

I look back at my life and ask myself, *what scares me?*
I can't build an army of clay… (I don't have the resources.)
But what I can do, is fuck my way through the gays of
Manchester. I can put notch after notch after notch on my
bedpost, and collect clay faces. I can remember the position
and shape of every pair of legs.

I don't think they'll fight for me when I'm gone.
But I'm not sure the terracotta troops fought for an ancient
Chinese corpse either.
He died alone, surrounded by statues and gold.
And I too, built an army.

03: YELLOW:

03.01:
Aureolin:

I survey my kingdom.
The fields that once bore wheats and grains. The orchards
that once yielded fruits. The corridors that once held
laughter and voices. Even this throne room, with its high,
reaching ceilings, rings hollow. My footsteps echo to the
tallest corners, booming out in rich, rolling thunderclaps. I
struggle to remember the music of my daughter's voice. The
rich anger of my son's bravado. The reassurance of my
wife's gentle laughter.

They are all gone now.
Instead I remain seated on my throne, surrounded by echoes.
All these golden statues; whose cold touch seems somehow
so familiar.

03.02:
Cadmium Yellow:

I will not break bread with you.
I will spill wine, not at your feet in libations,
But on your table, just to watch the stain set.
Five thousand more fish in the sea.

I bear open arms,
Without thinking,
Without expecting reward.
You bear a cross
And make every fucking moment of your suffering
An epic poem.

You wore false smiles until you forgot how to laugh.
I wore out the words 'I love you'.
You wore a mask.
I wore the t-shirt you slept in.
You wore a scarlet letter,
And I wore white.

I turn my back on you.
I am the doubting Thomas,
And your cock has crowed three times too many.
I shall kiss you on both cheeks and not mean it,
Whilst I watch you go.

I am Judas.
And there will be no second coming.

Amen.

03.03:
Canary:

I ask each one in turn, the same, politely phrased question. Their faces crinkle up in disbelief; they each struggle to comprehend how they found such kindness. After being crammed like cattle into train carriages and taken to Birkenau, with its imposing walls, and the towering chimneys of the crematoriums belching foetid smoke in the distance like stone dragons…

"Do you want to walk to the showers, or would you rather wait for the truck to take you?"

I don't ask them all. Some of them – the old, the crippled, the mentally impaired – they get ushered straight onto the trucks. As do most of the children; the intellectuals, the clergy, all the Romani gypsies, and any man suspected of being a homosexual.

I hand the rest the keys to their own prison with a simple question.
They will decide whether they too, are weak; or whether they will live.

03.04:
Citron:

The sand was so white and so fine, that to me it always seemed to be more like chalk dust. We used to walk hand in hand, kicking up clouds of it, staring out over a Mediterranean sunset, and you'd place your head on my shoulder and sigh so deeply, and so sweetly.

Now that I'm retired, and you're not quite who you used to be, we don't have the luxury of going to Naples any more. We can't quite relive our Honeymoon, or any of those glorious holidays from our youth.

But every year, like clockwork – on our anniversary; I pile sand at your feet and watch you trail your toes in the grains. I press sweet oranges and bitter lemons into your hands, and we smell the rinds, and we remember.

Oh, how we remember.

03.05:
Honey:

I can hear her through the walls and all she does is chew and eat and all I do is work and work and work and work and all I hear her do is chew and eat and give birth, kicking and screaming into the new world like a machine that only eats and chews and screams and clicks her mandibles and twitches her antennae and watches her children grow around her and serve and serve and work and work and drone and feed.

One day another one gave birth and laid her eggs and the eggs cracked open and brought new tiny buzzing claws into being and she grew angry and killed the children and killed the mother and grew fat and jealous and ate her royal jelly and sat in her splendour and watched us remove the bodies.

Jonquil:

I gathered flowers for you.
I climbed boughs in weighted skirts and reached for the
gentlest of blooms.
My arms heavy with martyred prayers and blossom,
Eventually the water had to take me.

I sang whilst I drowned.
My words were not in fear, nor alarm.
Song in white water and muddy depths.
Beauty even in the thrashing, flailing of a dying Ophelia,
Her trapt breaths release like music;

Crescendo.

Float,
Stagnant.

I gathered flowers for you.
I gathered skirts, heavy with drink,
And in disappearing cloud,
I, poor wretch, in melodious lay
Had to let the water take me.

I hate the way he chews with his mouth open.
I hate the way he corrects how I hold my knife and fork.
I hate how he eats his bacon nearly raw.
I hate the wet sounds it makes as he masticates noisily.
With his mouth open.

I hate how heavily he uses the ketchup.
I hate how he criticises how much salt I use.
I hate how he puts mustard on everything.
I hate how the smell lingers on his breath when he snores.
With his mouth open.

One of these days,
I will reach my breaking point.
And I will stab him in the neck with my fork until he can't
possibly chew any more.
Until he can't possibly swallow.
Not with his throat open.

I'm just nad about the new girl at school. There's something different about her. The way she puts safety-pins in her uniform and idly stabs her finger with her compass in double Maths.

Call me crazy, but Saffron… She might be mad about me. Today, she asked me if she could borrow a pen. I gave her my Parker. It has a steel finish and a gold-coloured barrel and writes like a dream. I got it for my fourteenth birthday. She used it to colour in her fingernails during English.

She chews gum and pops it loudly in Registration.
She wears her skirt higher than she's allowed to. I caught a flash of red satin when she uncrossed her legs in French.

I spend Lunch furiously wanking in a toilet stall. I ejaculate noisily over my hand, the seat and the inside of the lid.

…I'm just mad about Saffron…

I start again.

03.09:
Sulphur:

It happened before I could stop it.
No amount of buttock clenching would cage this beast. All I
could do was close my eyes and hope and pray that it was
silent. That it might not smell of anything.

It landed in the middle of a particularly poignant silence. A
muffled trumpet that skidded and squeaked its way through
the air between us; finishing in a particularly soggy-sounding
finale.

The interviewer paused mid-question. His nose twitched,
and his lips pursed slightly. The woman on his left held a
steely gaze. The man on his right tried vainly not a smile.

Then the stench came. Putrid, rotting eggs and cheap
microwavable meals tucked into a garbage fire. His eyes
watered, and he started dry-heaving.

…I let myself out.

03.10:
Sunflower Yellow:

We got off at Embankment. I don't know why it's called that. It seems such a silly name. But I like the way it fills my mouth like warm bread. It was busy, and I held Miss Carlton's hand tightly as we went through the ticket barriers; and up a long sloping street.

I'd never been inside a gallery before. I went to a museum once, but it only had clothes and arrowheads in glass cases and they were all brown and stone and dull.

I looked at all the faces in the paintings and they looked back at me and we didn't blink. But they were boring.

Then, there it was; just like in the picture-books. It was beautiful. I looked at the big yellow flowers in the vase and smiled brightly.

Then I opened my satchel, took out my crayons, and started to draw.

03.11:
Titan Yellow:

We watched the city burn from our balcony. Three of us,
knuckles white on the railing, watching the trail spread from
the Thames.
A tall shape, a shadow against the wheel.

There was a dull, yet constant screaming. Panic filled the air
like smoke, billowing out until it filled every available space,
and settling thick over the rooftops.

Sirens in unison.
The crashes of cars colliding.
Sparks from a fallen pylon.
A tower collapsed, and dust poured into the streets in tides.
And through it all, something thrashed.
Something huge.

I felt her grip tighten.

What is that thing?

It answered us with a roar.

Circled advert, glossy rag,
Seductive voice, curious call.
Magic words, magic number,
Magic marker, used bills.
He likes the way I sound.

Curled lashes, smoky eyes,
Red lips, lollipop smile.
Long legs, high heels,
Short skirt, black suspenders.
He likes the way I look.

Warm hands, cold eyes,
Soft curls, hard smile.
Strong walk, stronger gaze,
Harsh grip, strict rules.
He likes the way I move.

Ex-girlfriends, femme fatale.
Mother's milk, pink champagne.
Cherry stones, ripened fruit,
Inserted finger, moistened lips.
He likes the way I taste.

Spread legs, hiked skirt.
No panties, heavy breathing.
Cold sweat, warm stream,
Wide eyes, wider smile.
He likes the way I feel.

04. GREEN:

04.01:
Acid Green:

We spoke on and off for nearly three years. We even had an anniversary for our first conversation. And perhaps, due to circumstance, or maybe just fate; we never met.
I fell in love with the shape of your face in a handful of pictures; only dreamt what your voice might sound like in my ear, whispering from the other pillow.

We never called. Just typed. We were never single at the same time. It was just one of those things.

But three years on, we finally took the plunge. After you teased me with the open nature of your last love, before it gracelessly and abruptly ended.
We met, and spoke, and kissed between flat pints of Guinness. I learned you had an Irish accent. You saw I dyed my hair. It was a good night.

Two days later, a simple text.

I don't think it's going to work out. I had a nice time, but it's not for me. I don't think we've even got enough in common to be friends.

I deleted your number. I rejected your apologies.
Go to Hell.

04.02:
Jade:

My eyes are all over her hands.

Like wolves searching for the weakest deer to hunt.
I search for her vulnerability. She turns her wrist most
delicately, as she has been taught, and pulls back the sleeve
of her kimono.

It is decorated in persimmon fruit, and cherry blossoms.
She is gold and jade on the outside, milk and perfumed
honey on the inside.

Serve the men.
Don't make eye contact.
Until we grip your painted face.
For it is our right.

She will be mine.
I must have her, as a rich man must have the most precious
of jewels. I will buy her and own her and keep her shielded
from other eyes.

She makes me grow hard.

My eyes are all over her.

04.03:
Jungle Green:

She is Mami Wata. Mama Dlo. Mammadjo.
She is La Sirène. River Maiden. Mamba Muntu.
L'Amanté. Makanga. Madre de agua.

She, the nourishment of the bayou. She is the delta to the
swamps. She is the river that feeds the land. She nurses hills
from her rich ebon bosom. She is the stock that swims
amongst broken chicken necks.

She can be life. But she can be death.

She hangs the ribcages of those who trespass, from the low-
hanging branches. She is a strange, poisonous fruit. She
threads the hearts of unfaithful men.

She can be death. But she can be kind.

She fills the wombs of barren mothers. She helps those who
seek beauty find it in their hand mirrors. She is the waters of
life. She is the eternal snake goddess. She is the death of
vanity. The death of want. The death of need.

She is.
She simply is.

04.04:
Laurel Green:

I watched over you while you slept.
I kept, I kept, I kept, I kept
A vigil long and deep;
I watched you in your sleep.

You held me on nights you were scared
Of monsters underneath your bed,
Of branches rat-tat-tat-ing on the glass
Like bony fingertips.
You squeezed me when you heard the sounds
Behind your closet door.
When floorboards creaked in the midnight hour.
You looked into my button eyes
For safety when you were small.

Now that you've grown,
I only serve to gather dust
On shelves next to other relics
Of your childhood.
I once protected you from ghouls and goblins and demons.
But now I can only watch you fight
The battles I could never have prepared you for.

Your first broken heart.
The day you tried to swallow all those pills.
When your boyfriend got cancer.
The day your father died.
The day you burned his body.

And I know there's more to come.
But these button eyes can't shed tears.

04.05:
Mantis:

I wrap my thighs around his neck, and clench.
The spasms are rippling through me.
And I am a pond whose surface is no longer mirror still.
I am an ocean, whose waves lap at the beach
As greedily as his tongue is lapping at my clit,
Flicking in tidal strokes,
Making me clutch the pillow in ways I forgot I could.

Cunnilingus. Say it with me now.
Cunn-i-ling-us.

I press his face into me,
Pretend he is a starving man
In desperate need of a ham sandwich.
I feel his teeth, but I don't mind.
His beard scratches something awful.
It tickled at first, but his chin is rubbing me raw.
But God! – His mouth is magic.

When I finally come,
Bucking sharply and fiercely,
Squirting juices over his teeth,
Making him swill me like mouthwash,
I imagine him eating dates.
Scooping the flesh with his fat, swollen tongue,
And savouring its bittersweetness.

I catch my breath, sit up against the pillows.
He is not moving.
His collarbones are jutting out of his neck
Like knitting needles poking through scarlet wool.

They paid me well. Handsomely, even.
And it wasn't as if we were married, or if we'd really said much of anything to each other.
But he trusted me.
Three times I asked, and three times he lied, until I needled the truth out of him. I always get what I want. I am a most determined woman.

I fucked him.
I let him sow his seed deep inside me, and when he lay sleeping afterwards, his head in my stained lap; I bared those scissors like a holy rod. I cut off his locks, cropped close to the temple, and watched the Philistines gouge out his eyes in penance.

They paid me well. And now I am rich.
I will one day bear a son, and the books won't remember our names. We will be forgotten, but well looked after.

I won't listen on the winds for news of his punishments.
And I won't ever be sorry.
I won't ever let a man control me again.

4.07:
Paris Green:

I watched my homeland shrink.

Like I watched beautiful women shrink in my presence.
They clutch themselves and try to hide within the hollows of
their own faces.
It is a mixture of fear and envy and hatred.
They feel lesser.
Unused to being the second brightest light in the room, they
huddle in corners when I enter.
I am a paragon, but I am not proud of this fact.

Greece disappeared on the horizon.
I thought of the curves of Menelaus' face.
He would miss me.
He would hate me.
He would both desire and detest my womanhood, my
audacity.
But Paris?
He waits for me in Troy.

And I would gladly let the continent burn.
Would gladly let my husband send a thousand of his ships if
it helps him see
Who I truly love now.

Somehow you always managed to keep it all together. Even living under your parents wings, not even daring to emerge from the closet for fear of being disowned.

Whilst I was ten years into my own freedom, struggling to make ends meet in dead end jobs and sleeping under squalid roofs. You were trying to be a model.

You coasted on being pretty and slightly dumb, and so naive that after you moved to London, you were so wrapped up in discovering bills for the first time my suicide attempt went largely unnoticed.

Now you have a good job, a rich doctor on your arm, and a decent place in the capital. You spend your time collecting stamps on your passport and taking selfies with designer Easter eggs.

It should have been my life. I did all the legwork. Instead I'm peddling stories in the back rooms of pubs, faking that I've got something to say.

You're no longer trying to make it as a model. But the thought does little to comfort me.

04.09:
Racing Green:

My father always taught me to treat a woman like a vintage car. With caution, care, and a delicate hand.

Don't push her too hard. Mind the curves of her body, and treat her with respect.

I'd climb inside them to smell them. Inhale the leather interiors and stroke the velvet linings. But never use them. Never drive them. Never fill the engines.
Just maintain them. Keep them for show.

Nothing looks better than a vintage car on the driveway. It intimidates business partners when you engineer visits to your house. And it's always impressive to own.

When you get bored of them, when you've replaced all their parts, you sell them. And move on to the next project.

04.10:
Sap Green:

Earth mother.
Mother Earth.

Feel it in your root.
Deep inside your belly,
Somewhere behind the moment where your hips cracked
And another life was dragged,
Kicking and screaming into being.
You bled for a long time,
And shallow-pan-fried your placenta.

You called her Gaia,
Because she was beautiful.
And because she was glorious.
And you lay with her in meadows,
Feeling grass beneath your skin.

You hugged oak trees,
Just to make the suits angry.
Felt the bark chafe your skin
And knew that it was good.
Saw that it was good.

Hold your belly.
Find your root.
Leak sap on the meadows,
Feel it slide between your toes
And know that it is time
For another labour of love.

A mother's work is never done.

04.11:
Seafoam:

Tell me what you're looking for?

It's phrased as a question, but it isn't. It's a cry for help.
Tears are streaming down her face, and I can see that she's
hurting. She wants me to come inside. She wants to
understand. But I cannot.
Not just yet.

I watch the waves. I watch them crash against the rocks far
below me, dispersing into flecks of foam and spray and mist.
It is beautiful. But does nothing to quell the seething inside
me.

Tell me what you really need?

I just want to watch the ocean.
Go away, my love.
Leave me with my thoughts. I need to put them in line, re-
order my demons before they beckon me.
Before I finally take the plunge.

04.12:
Spring Green:

I killed him that day.
I took him in my arms and strangled the life out of him; the
day Anita was born. I buried blue baby clothes and action
figures in a locked box.

When they ask you what it was like when you came out, you
say 'I always knew'. But I had to kill him to live like her.

Anita has no past. Only a future.
Anita was never a little girl in her mother's size six heels,
pretending to be a woman.
Anita never existed before the age of thirty-one.
Anita was born a fully grown woman, a living, breathing
woman.
Anita will die a woman. A living, breathing woman.

But he…
He died many years ago.
He has no future.
And he will not be remembered.
Not even his sacrifices.

05.01:
Alice Blue:

I'm struggling to remember.
I get snatches. Watercolour scenes that float across my
vision in sepias tones. I'm wearing my blue dress.

I ran;
Followed the white rabbit.

Rewinding clocks and bottles labelled '*drink me*'.
Mock turtles crying an ocean of tears. A smiling cat; a
scarecrow. A creature stitched together from parts of
memories and lives that I can't quite recall. Shades of times
and places.
Hearts, jam tarts, a tin-man and a yellow brick road.
Flamingos wearing ruby slippers, and my dress is still blue.

The storm of the century; a flying house and a castle full of
monkeys, and I don't know if this is my life. Are these mine?
…Memories or just dreams? It smells of toast. Wet sponges
on the side of my head. A wooden rod between my teeth.
More clocks, dials, sparks.

I don't know who I am.
I don't know who I am.
Idon'tknowwhoIamwhoamIIamwhoIambutwhoamIIdon'tknowwhoIam
whoamIwhoamIwhoamI?

He cries.
…Of course he does. He's a baby.

And I hate myself for thinking of him as anything less than my child, but sometimes I catch myself.
He'll never be normal.

And he cries.
And I cry.

I can't tell whether he lives day to day in physical pain. But he screams when I touch him.

His physical therapy wounds me; cuts deep. I massage his legs, and bend his limbs and try not to make eye contact with this crushed up, wailing changeling.

In the evenings when he is quiet, I drift into dreamscapes where he grows up healthy. Where he is able. I fidget with corners of blankets, and imagine if I'd be happier had I found the nerve to keep that clinic appointment.

I'm a horrible person.
A terrible mother.
I spend so much time listening to him cry, that I'm scared I'll never hear him laugh.

05.03:
Dayflower:

It's been six years and I've only just taken his pictures down.
I've tried to be so careful, but every week turns up another relic.
Another knife under the ribs.
Another hook.

I always thought he'd leave me. That one day, he'd realise I wasn't good enough, and march into the kitchen, a stern look in his eyes… and serve me papers over the morning coffee.

But he never did.
Of course, when he died; suddenly; in the street. Without warning, or cause…
I was quietly relieved.

But it wasn't like I had anything better to do.
Except wait.

I have my first date with Vernon tonight. I'm nervous, but quietly giddy. It's like I'm sixteen again, and the last thirty years of marriage have been swept clear. The table has been reset.
But I know he'll ask about Robert. And when he does, the spark will die.

…It always does.

05.04:
Electric Blue:

It was like swimming through a sea of needles.
One hundred thousand million tiny pinpricks tapping at my
skin. The sensation of every hair on my arm being
individually, yet simultaneously tweezed.

I could be flying.
That this feeling was the breeze rushing over my skin as I
soared; propelled by the blast. That this moment
encapsulated the experience of the birds; drafts catching the
underside of their feathers. Every quill being individually, yet
simultaneously tugged by a wayward wind.

I was a dancer spinning in slow, deliberate circles. Part of an
underwater ballet. The denouement of Swan Lake. Under
the surface, watching with wide open eyes, blinking in
murky water.

I felt all of this.
But from the outside; I suspect it looked entirely different.

From the outside, a lone figure simply got struck by
lightning, and crumpled to the ground, smoking like a burnt
out match.

05.05:
Forget-Me-Not:

I'm in love with a dying man…
I'm in love with a dying man…
I'm in love with a dying man…
I'm in love with a dying man.

I'm in love with a dying man…
I'm in love with a dying man…
I'm in love with a dying man…
I'm in love with a dying man.

I'm in love with a dying man…
I'm in love with a dying man…
I'm in love with a dying man…
I'm in love with a dying man.

I'm in love with a dying man…
I'm in love with a dying man…
I'm in love with a dying man…
I'm in love with a dying man.

There's a rhythm to this city at night. Tiny eyes peering out from alleyways that we never knew existed. Nooks largely forgotten and ignored by those who walk the streets in the day.

There's a hidden music in this town. Bats sweep the skies and clutch moths in greedy teeth. Foxes forage through bins and cry like infants; through mouths of burger wrappers and half-picked kebabs.

There's beauty in the dark in this place. Rats trace a hidden pilgrimage through waterways and gutters. Pigeons squat and stain every surface. Beetles infest everything. Woodlice under rocks, centipedes winding lover's knots, and cockroaches booking out every hotel.

Everything looks grey.
But it hums with life, if we'd only look. Scratch at the dirty veneer. Under the surface, there's a brilliant hue.

A beating blue-grey heart.

05.07:
Maya Blue:

Dance with me?

She wore a kinda leather catsuit unzipped to her navel.
Her hair was sorta long and dark to match her skin.
She was clearly going bra-less and quite possibly had magical
tit-tape.
She moved like water.

You're not like all the other lipsticks here...

I found myself staring at her belly.
Occasionally she'd clutch it as she danced,
Writhing as if she weren't quite familiar with her own limbs,
But simply didn't care.

It's so fucking hot in here...

Pulling down her zipper a little further;
A small symbol etched on her skin,
Just above the danger zone.
Her cunt.

A shiny red apple.

Just
One
Bite.

05.08:
Morning Glory:

I fucked him in the bathroom stall.
The trade.
With the classic chiselled chin and closely-cropped crew-cut.
A white t-shirt and low-riding jeans.

I heard guys doing blow on the other side of the partition;
Off a urine-caked cistern.
Drag-queens reading aloud snatches of 4a.m. confessions
Scrawled on the backs of doors
That didn't lock, so much as wedge shut.

I took swigs from neon blue bottles between thrusts.
I came inside him as he gripped the top of the door,
The hinges banging and rattling to the cheers and jeers
Of those waiting to piss in the trough.
Someone stubbed a cigarette out on the tip of his index finger.

He followed me home even though I said no.
Crawled into the same taxi from a different door.

We didn't talk on the way back,
Didn't even make eye contact.

I woke alone with a hard-on
And his number written on my arm in black marker.

It had smudged in my sleep.

_05.09:_
Powder Blue:

Everything burns a little bit brighter
And the colours all turn a bit lighter,
And when I blink they only grow
And glow
And gleam and sheen and shine.

Catch a buzz, and feel renewed,
The colours strengthen good as new,
And greens are slightly pink and blue
And gold
And red and never black.

People talk but they don't really say anything.
Lips move, cheeks chew,
And saliva washes around their faces
Like the spin cycle at the laundromat.
Just add sugar;
And they make music.
Poetry.
They spread the word of God,
Midnight masses.
Gospels at 3a.m. in takeaway joints,
Talking in tongues over chips drowning in gravy.

At home,
I dream in black and white.
I dream I sit in a cubicle and sharpen pencils
One by one.
And I wake with the body of Christ on my tongue;
A tab to bring the coloured flames
Come dancing back.

05.10:
Pure Blue:

Toxins.
Nasty chemicals. Bad chemicals. All chemicals are bad.
Toxins.

Oil.

Scented snake oil. Organic rape seed oil. Unprocessed virgin coconut oil. Lubricant for the soul.
Now on sale.

Evil.
Evil corporations. Mass-market. Scientifically tested.
Toxins.

Wonderful.
Exfoliating scrub. Boutique prices. Good for you. Celebrity endorsements.
Five stars.

Conspiracy.
Vaccinations cause autism. Jet fuel can't melt steel beams.
Science.
Evil.

Cleansing.
Clarify your aura. Realign your chakra. Centre your yoni.
Homeopathic supplements.
Buy now.

05.11:
Royal Blue:

Put your hands on me.
Touch me like you used to.
Nowadays, we don't even talk.
Words left unsaid fill the void
Between our bodies in our separate beds,
When we watch each other's mouths
From opposite ends of the table.
Chewing,
Just chewing.
Opening and closing,
Talking in wet sounds
But never listening.

Touch me.
Lay hands on me.
Make the hairs on my skin
Prick
At the very nearness of you.
Even the slightest brush
Or
With an open palm
Or
A closed fist.
Colour me black and royal blue if you have to.

Just acknowledge;
Pretend for a day
That
I
Am
Here.

Vista Blue:

I wish I looked up more.

I grew up in a rough part of London,
Where every street
Had a broken sheet of concrete;
Where iron tips leaned in
To steal kisses from your shins and knees and ankles.

We used to walk along those ledges all the time.
Twisted rebars and broken lines.
We used to balance on industrial beams and play pretend.

One day a girl in the year below
Tripped and knocked out four teeth.
It took them weeks
To clean up the blood.
We had to go over the chalk marks
In certain parts,
So we could play hopscotch with all the numbers.

I spent my childhood watching my tiptoes.
Making sure I never slipped, though
I walked into more walls and lamp-posts
Than any other child in our school.

Now that I've found my feet,
I look out.
To wherever this road may take me.
To the future.
But some days, I wish I were a dreamer.
And that I could just watch the clouds go by.

06: PURPLE:

06.01:
Aniline:

Had she done something wrong?

Her neighbours had all gone.
Her family.
Her husband.
…Even her children.

They had all left her.

She was alone;
She was the residue in the bottom of the glass.
The dried milk.

She looked up at the clouds and wondered

Why her?

Would they come back for her eventually?
Was it a mistake?
Was she simply not ready?

She sat on a kerb, and counted her sins.
Too dumbfounded to be sad. Too confused to be lonely.
She wondered if the Rapture might come around a second
time, and if then, she might be worthy.

06.02:
Cornflower:

They think I don't hear what they say about me, but they forget how far my influence reaches. They scurry amongst the ziggurats, between fields of failing maize, and they panic. They whisper behind closed doors and conspiratorial palms.

He asks for too much.
The feathered serpent dooms us all.
Are all Gods this terrible?

And I smile with thin lips, even though they cannot see. And for every complaint, for every fearful remark, I simply add more to the toll.

I will be sated.
I can keep this up forever. I can ask for more than gold, more than cereal harvest. And the more they fear, the more they hate me, the more I'm tempted to see what exactly they will supplicate me with...

Our children will starve.

...or whom.

06.03:
Eggplant:

#NoPicNoChat
#NoTimeWasters
#NoFats
#NoFemmes
#NoAsians
#ItsNotRacismItsAPreference
#NotIntoBlack
#NotIntoCamp
#Str8ActingOnly
#Masc4Masc
#TopForBottom
#OlderForYounger
#BoyForDaddy
#CleanOnly
#PozOnly
#DiseaseFree
#HungOnly
#8+Only
#PigsOnly
#BBOnly
#RawSlut
#BreedMe
#FeedMe
#MusclesToTheFrontOfTheQueue
#TranniesNeedNotApply
#Over30sNeedNotApply
#SaneAndSortedOnly
#FriendsOnly
#MeetsOnly
#LosingMessages
#DontTakeItPersonally

I always wanted grandchildren.

To be specific, I always wanted a granddaughter. A little girl with bouncing blonde ringlets; someone I could dress up in frilly dresses and ribbons. A beautiful princess I could spoil with all the things I could never give her mother.

A chance to correct a lifetime of poverty. Where grafting to put food on the table was more important than seeing her first step. Or hearing her first word.

If I ever leave this hospital, I will make Gwen promise me that she will have a baby. And that she'll name her after me. It might be an old fashioned name – nobody ever heard of a child called Gertrude, or Mavis, or Ruth any more.

They dip in and out of fashion like the lengths of skirts. Now we have a generation named Apple and Ocean and Khaleesi.

…whatever that is.

I don't understand it myself.

06.05:
Lavender:

She told me she was a witch and I believed her.

She had beguiled me with her looks, her charms and her kisses.
She brought out the Wiccan in me, made me howl at the moon
and paint my eyes in darker shades.
She made me believe in myself.
She made me feel desired and capable of desire.
She made me feel like a strong woman.
She soothed my aches and pains.
She rubbed my shoulders when they were sore, and kissed
my feet.
She told me she would wash them with her hair if it would
make me happy.
She held my stomach when I cramped.
She stroked my face whilst I slept.

She left lavender on my pillows, and I always woke happy.

We never argued.
We never screamed.
I felt like we did, but somehow, somewhere, I forgot.
The arguments just got lost.

06.06:
Maroon:

Press my ear up against your empty chest.
Strain to hear a beat.
Knock, and it's hollow.

We're not dead, we didn't die.
Our love must still be here somewhere.
Stoke the embers.
Sift the beaches until we rediscover an old diamond,
Once thought lost.
Can't swallow any more rocks so I chew sand instead.
Grit in my teeth, stones in my shoe.
Listen out for prayers in the dead of night;
They're like waves crashing,
Receding with the hours.

I'm still, but I'm not at ease.

The dishonesty on your breath almost
As strong as the whiskey almost
As rancid as her perfume.
A bitter fruit filled with ashes
That left tar on my tongue,
And stuck my lips together.

I cannot show weakness.
I can't tell you how scared I am to be alone.
How I fear one day I'll simply walk into the sea and
Disappear.

Disposing of a body is a delicate operation. It requires the fingers of a surgeon; and the calculations of a genius mathematician.

Even a wayward neighbour taking out the bins at an inopportune moment can throw the whole thing off – derailed by unexpected traffic, or a nosy mother-in-law. Alibis, keeping up appearances, having the right tools for the job… It's an art. Everything must be planned down to the last exacting detail. Or the game's over. Lost before it ever really started.

I don't usually do this sort of thing.
You know, you hear about this kind of stuff all the time.
Girl goes back to a strange man's place… ends up all over the news for weeks after.
Did you hear about that student that got raped a few streets down? …mental.
…Not that I'm implying you'd…
…sorry.
I've made an ass of myself, haven't I?
(Stop talking Karen – take your foot out of your mouth for once.)
You know we've been chatting for quite a while now…
I really like you.
It's been nice finding someone I can really connect to.
I mean, we have so much in common, it's scary.
…I think my parents would really like you.

She laughs.

06.08:
Pansy:

Fag. Faggot. Fairy. Flamer.
Fruit. Gay. Homo. Nancy.
Pansy. Pervert. Ponce. Poof.
Poofter. Queer. Sissy. Sodomite.

Arse-bandit. Batty-boy.
Bum-boy. Cock-sucker.
Gay-boy. Limp-Wrist.
Shirt-lifter. Shit-stabber.

Man up.
Don't be such a girl.
God Hates Fags.
Just fucking die.

Man the fuck up.
Don't be such a fucking girl.
God Fucking Hates Fags.
Just fucking die.

Backs to the walls.
Don't drop the soap.

Get out of this house.
Don't come back.

Do you have a lighter?

I have a third eye and it can see inside you and it tells me
that you are beautiful and afraid and not quite willing to
accept that people might find you attractive and
do you have a lighter?

My hands see much more than my eyes and when I touch
you I feel scars and see the ways in which you are scarred
and the ways in which you are scared and the way you want
to hide and still be seen and
do you have a lighter?

I touch myself and look at myself and explore the intimate
curves of my own body and where I go in and where I go
out and where I might be more than I want and where I
seem too small and
do you have a lighter?

I am rarely comfortable in my own skin even though I am
well practised at pretending and you feel the same and
together we could be like music if you would only let us and
do you have a lighter?

06.10:
Tyrian Purple:

He begs me to choke him.
He pleads for me to grab him by the hair.
To spit on his face and in his mouth.
He wants to be hit. To be slapped. To be punished.
He wants to feel alive.

He calls me 'Sir'.
He calls me 'Master'.
He calls me 'Daddy.'
He never uses my name.
I validate his existence, but I'm not a person to him. Not
really. I'm a means to an end.

He likes to have scratch marks left down his back.
He likes to be bitten.
His eyes fill with wonder when he holds my hands around
his throat.
He likes me to leave handprints on his arse-cheeks.
He loves me when I leave handprints on his face.

He wants me to fuck his face until he cries.
He wants to be raped.

He wonders why I can't look him in the eye when I pass
him the salt.
I wonder why I stay.

06.11:
Ultraviolet:

I cut off all my hair one day.
I used kitchen scissors, dirty from last night's chicken to hack away at myself.

I tore holes in my favourite t-shirt, and went to college wearing it without a bra. I enjoyed it when my nipples occasionally kissed the city air. I let the stares wash over me.

I wore an old padlock, left closed and key lost, on a chain around my neck. I drew temporary tattoos on my forearms with a blue biro.

I burned all my old pictures.
I wanted to erase her from history.
That shy, retiring girl with the meek voice and no confidence.

I stamped her out.
I was here to stay.
This was my body now, and I wasn't letting go.

Dear Diary;
Only you know how I'm unable to recognise faces. People's
features swim in and out of my vision and drift away like
cigarette smoke.
I've learned to cope – I use clothes and hairstyles and the
certain way people walk to recognise them. The way they
hold themselves.

This clique at my school seem to have made it easier for me.
Whether it's a conscious choice or not, they insist on only
wearing variations of one colour each.

Red is Queen Bee. She wears the sacred scrunchies of power
and stands like a Spartan. She's unflinching and reeks of
high-school Hubris… What's her damage?
Green is the seat of all envy. She's quiet and generally quite
nice when Red isn't around. But she's a diet-coke-head – a
jealous lapdog waiting to bite the hand that feeds.
Yellow is timid. She's mousey and cowardly (for a
cheerleader) and mostly pretends she's not listening.
Sometimes she acts like she had a brain tumour for
breakfast. She's the nicest of the three.

I was drawn to them because of my condition. Because of
the poetry of it all. And now I'm trapped.

Dear Diary;
I don't really like my friends.

07. PINK:

07.01:
Barbie Pink:

Bend me, shape me.
Any way you want me.
I can stand, or kneel for you or get on all fours.
I am your living, breathing doll.
I'm double-jointed in all the right places.
I'm thin in all the right places.
I only have curves where you want them.
I'm wet where you need me.

I only have hair on my head.
Long, blonde locks down to my waist.
No hair on my face.
No hair on my arms.
No hair on my legs.
No hair on my pussy.
I'm smooth all over.
I'm practically plastic for you.

You can dress me how you see fit.
Pick out my shoes, pick out my dress.
Tell me if you want me to go commando.
Tell me if you want me barefoot.
Tell me if you want me wearing only heels.

I love to be used.
I love to be owned.
Never let me go.

Cameo Pink:

Count me in.

Four. Three. Two. One.
Feel the rhythm, hear the drums.

Arms, legs – Give face.
Bend, flex – Give face.
Strike pose – Give face.
Dance bitch, – And give me face!

One. Two. Three.
Strike a pose for me.
One. Two. Three.
Hold that pose for me.
One. Two. Three.
Snatch that weave for free.
One. Two. Three.
Watch, repeat; after me.

Arms, legs – Give face.
Bend, flex – Give face.
Strike pose – Give face.
Dance bitch, – And give me face!

Vogue. Show. Fast. Slow.
Rattle dem limbz. Rhythms and hymns.
Drop it down, earn that crown.
Spill the tea; don't come for me!
Cameo? Steal the show!
Be a diva, and dance, bitch!

Count me out.

07.03:
Champagne Pink:

Wake up in a different bed again and look for my knickers
but I just cannot see them where are they and where are my
shoes there's one on the bedside lamp and the other is
somewhere I cannot see.

Tiptoe to the bedroom door and let myself out but help
myself to your Rolex and a tenner from your wallet for the
taxi and I still haven't found my panties and I'm not even
sure which ones I wore out are they red or pink or blue?

In the hallway mirror I see my mascara has spread out over
my face like a panda and I have to divert to the kitchen and
down half a bottle of Moet just to catch my breath and I
rinse my face under the tap but it just doesn't shift.

I go through my handbag and I snort another key of coke
whilst I wait for the taxi and upstairs I hear an alarm going
off and so I let myself out and smoke a cigarette.

When I finally get home my mother and father and all of my
friends and that guy I've been shagging for nearly six
months now even though I don't want a relationship are all
in my lounge and they tell me that they want to help and sit
me down.

I start to cry.

Copper:

I wore pretty underwear,
Hoping you might take it off.

When I finally mustered up the courage,
Finally found the word 'No' on my tongue
You punched me in the mouth.
Ignored my feeble protest.
I wanted it really—
It was obvious, you said.
Another fist; the taste of copper fills my mouth.
You hold me down.

I wore pretty underwear,
Hoping you might take it off.

My face is on fire and filled with shards of burning metal.
I blink away more tears,
Blink through another trickle of blood.
Another torrent.
My nose this time – Is it broken?
I am outside myself,
Watching two men fuck in a darkened room;
Anger and pity.
This isn't happening to me, I think.
His toes curl.
He wipes himself off on my pillow.
His boots take the longest time to lace back up.
The stench of him fills the room, even after he leaves.

I wore pretty underwear,
Hoping you might take it off.

07.05:
Flesh:

Dig my fingers in.

Feel the flow beneath your skin. Feel the hairs prick at my penetrative touch. My invasion. Learn the way your body moves, the way your flesh crawls. How does your blood run – in rivers or stagnant pools? Does it gush, or seep, or slide like oil?

When I have gleaned the habits of your coil, learned how you adapt to my foreign body; I can begin my work. I am inside you so much; you are nearly more me than you.

I can shape you in ways you never imagined. I will break you down, build you back up. Construct cartilage and mutilate bone.

You come to me, because you hate the way you look; and I will change you. I won't always make you beautiful. I won't always make you distinguished.

Sometimes I'm just finger-fucking you in an alley, until you emerge from the shadows, a blinking monster.

He's a slag. He's had more pricks than 'Ker-plunk'.
His erogenous zones are more like regions.
His Bermuda triangle is less of a tightly clenched shape and
more of a… gaping canyon.

I'm not slut-shaming though. He's a slut.
He is. He knows it, we know it – everyone knows it.
He wears it proudly.
On his sleeve, like a badge.

Him and his pink triangle.

They don't make him wear it any more.
They don't parade him down a walk of fame;
Lined by yellow stars and velvet chains.
We took it back.
We reclaimed.
Flipped the script; turned the page;
Twisted the intention until we felt comfortable in our own
skins.
Until the words felt comfortable in our own mouths.

SILENCE=DEATH.

We survived your AIDs.
Your 'help'.
Your Christian suggestion.
Love thy neighbour.

And He?
He has more love to give, than anyone I've ever known.

Hannah isn't sick, not at all.
The doctors tried to do all these tests on her and threw lots
of their mumbo jumbo words around, but I don't need them
to pollute my head with all their clinical terms. I know she's
special, and always has been.

She's a teenager now, and she's just fine. Sometimes she has
difficulty walking, but I tell her that's because, as a star child,
she's carrying the weight of the world on her shoulders.
She's an empath, and bears the weight of all humanity's pain.

It's a heavy burden, and I wish I could share it for her. But
I'm just not blessed in the same way Hannah is. Some days
the sickness of the planet is too much for her, and she cries
blood and can't even feed herself.

But as mother to crystal-born, I know I too have my own
trials. I help her as best I can, spoon-feeding her in her
worst days, and helping her stand.

This world will kill her before she turns twenty. But she still
has so much goodness in her. So much compassion and
kindness to give. I will see to it, that she does so; every
bloodied footfall of the way.

I haven't had meat for twenty years. I've only ever slept with women, and I've never been curious about men. I played sports, and practised woodwork, and drank pints down the pub with mates.

All in all, I'd say I'm pretty masculine.

It started as a dare; a bit-part in a stag night. But now, I wear women's clothes on a regular basis. Heels, wigs, lashes, lipstick and three hours of foundation and contouring.

Not for my sake, but for hers.
Magenta.

She's a carnivore, through and through. She keeps her pantyhose in decorative eggs. She loves to get fucked from behind. She likes it when they rip her wig off in the heat of the moment, and spunk up inside her.

She's more than just that little voice in the back of my head now.
She's the reason I'm shitting blood and she's the reason why I've had more AIDS tests than hot meals.
She's the reason my wife no longer gets me hard.

I don't know who I am anymore.

My eyes are all over my body.

Like travellers searching for the weakest point to cross.
I discover all my vulnerability. I turn my wrist in disgust,
hide it as I've been taught; and pull back the sleeve of my
kimono.

It is decorated in persimmon fruit, and cherry blossoms.
I am gold and jade on the outside, but rot and decay on the
inside.

Pour the tea.
Don't make eye contact.
Hide behind your painted face.
For it is a mask.

I will be free.
I must have liberty, as a trapped man must have the most
glorious of breaths. I will fight and try and keep my head
down and earn my civility.

I will learn to be both hard and soft.

My eyes are always closed now.

As children, we are always in such a rush to grow up, and as adults, we clutch desperately at shades of our youth.

Seven-year old girls wearing a full face of make-up; barely able to lift their lids under caked layers of eyeshadow. The rouged smiles of babes.

Boys having pissing competitions, measuring their genitals and padding their underwear with balled-up gym socks. A competition for status symbols – the first pubic hair.

Life is short, cruel and hard.
No better living creature to ask than the salmon. It adapted to fresh and saltwater because so few of its eggs ever reach adulthood. It is slaughtered at every step; from pollution, to erratic water temperatures, to the harsh final reality of the bear's jaws. It constantly fights the tide, swimming upstream; up waterfalls if it has to.

Life is short, cruel and hard.
But only humans ever seem to learn this the hard way.
Only humans are convinced that we're entitled to the very opposite.

I don't think about the families of the prepubescent girls I have stripped and suspended in barbed wire cages. When I am as naked as they are, stood proudly beneath them as they bleed all over me, I only think of how they're giving the greatest gift of all. How selfless they are.

I will remain young forever; bathing in this virgin blood. This life force. The ichor sustains me, invigorates my skin and my flesh, and I deserve it.
I am better than these lowly waifs, and they, as part of my Kingdom and rule, must serve me in any way I deem necessary.

I value their sacrifice, when I break their bones to suck the pure marrow.
I value their sacrifice, when I flense the very skin from their quivering fat, and apply it liberally before sleep.
I love my people, and the people love me. They would do anything for me. And I would do anything to stay this way forever.

07.12:
Shocking Pink:

Fibres.
Wires. In the blood.
Fibre-optic cables in my flesh.

I pick them out with tweezers thinking it must be lint, but
they keep coming back.
Where are they coming from?

Under my microscope I see blood.
I see skin cells.
And fibres.

I collect them in a sterile test tube – the doc will want to see
them. Send them for study.

I itch.
Am I real?
Am I just plugged in?
Where are the fibres?
I can't see them and I'm scared I'm losing it.
There should be wires here.

I go searching.
I buy tools and go searching.

08.01:
Antique White:

Where's there's smoke,
There's heartbreak.
The clocks have all stopped at twenty to nine.

The wedding cake is perfect on the tarnished table.
The breakfast laid uneaten for a thousand hours.
My dress and all my finery have never looked finer,
A pity the same cannot be said about the bride.

The spark has lit in you.
Do you feel that you have lost her?
The clocks have all stopped at twenty to nine.

They call me the witch of the palace.
They tell me my heart is forged from ice.
They say I look like nothing but a bag of bones.
They think I'm naught but a waxwork fallacy.

The flames will consume me.
I forgive her.
The clocks have all stopped at twenty to nine.

The bitter taste of ashes.
The clocks have all stopped at twenty to nine.
The clocks have all stopped at twenty to nine.

<u>*08.02:*</u>
<u>*Cotton:*</u>

There's a history of mental illness in the family? On the maternal side, yes?

…My Grandmother. We used to say she 'had a season ticket to Wonderland.'

It's hardly a death sentence. Nowadays there are a variety of treatments—

Isn't this the part where you tell me that these hallucinations are a gift? That I'm special? The 'Chosen One'? Magic, and gatekeepers and all that shit? There's supposed to be something. A radioactive spider. An origin story. I should get powers – I have to! You see it all the time on the telly.

No.

Tell me there's more to this? …Lie to me…

You'll be fine. No need to worry.

Hard-ball it, Doc. I won't break; I'm not made of glass.

There are no demons to slay here. You are not Chosen. You're very ordinary. Unluckily ordinary…

And mad? Oh Doc… We're all mad here. But only some of us know it…

<u>**08.03:**</u>
<u>**Cream:**</u>

Boobs.
Boobs, boobs, boobs.
Boooooooooooooooobs.

Mammaries. Breasts. Fun bags. Sweaty, meaty, milk-glands.

Tits.

I fucking love 'em.
I literally cannot get enough of boobs. Big boobs, small boobs, boobs in-between. Coat-hooks, pillow cases, chesticles and mountain ranges, ironing boards and bee-stings…
My love for boobs is infinite.
I don't discriminate.

I love leaky boobs the most.
Leaky boobs, seep-y boobs, dairy boobs and weepy boobs.

I find the idea of cows being milked strangely, but only faintly erotic.
I think nursing bras are fucking hot.
I think nipple shields are the worst things to ever happen to the civilised world.
Breast pumps are my sex toys.

I think the thought of seeing a woman strolling around with an undone button (or three), no bra, a pair of barely-contained life-buoys bobbing up for air; and *two glorious damp patches*…
Well. That's a fucking wet dream.

That's fucking perfect.

08.04:
Eggshell:

She hasn't noticed it yet.

In her relief, she is more concerned with getting as far from the planet's surface as possible. Away from the doomed rescue craft.
Away from the bodies strung up amongst the fluorescent lights by their intestines.

She hasn't noticed it yet.

It tucks itself away discreetly.
It has no wish to be seen, to be discovered. Hidden beneath a never-used monitor, behind a crate of provisions. And it learns to throb in time with the ship's engines.
It learns to pulse with the beat of the motors.
It cracks to the tune of a distant dying star.

It will crack her neck the same way; sucking fluids from her spine like a mother's milk.

But mother, I've never ridden a horse before…

Her gaze is fixed, her jaw slightly agape. And she has never looked more innocent. The way she curiously, but gingerly pets the beast on his jaw, twirling her fingers in his mane.

How will I know if I like it?

It is then, that I catch the sweeping movements of her eyes, and I know she will. I can see how she'll take to it, and flourish. She examines the tight sinews of the horse's body. The thick flanks, and powerful legs. Her gaze transforms from amazement, to adoration, to something else. Something hungrier.
And she watches his strong muscles ripple, and she's lost in a reverie. She bites her lip, strokes his face, and stares into his eyes.

She sees it too. She'll love her first stallion as much as I did. A forbidden, untamed love. Just like her mother's.

My favourite chair is my life's work. The hides of three different animals, leather worn by the elephant, the rhinoceros and the hippopotamus, all stitched together in a knotted, creased work of art.
It's back is made from intricately carved tusks – ripped from the corpses of four warthogs and a bull elephant. And when I am splayed across its arms, marvelling at my trophies, I feel like primordial man. I feel powerful. I am a God.

But one day, I know there will come a knocking at my door. I will answer it, and be found wanting. I will face a jury of ghostly eyes, each blinking through a bloodied visage. Each bearing the stigmata of the hunt.

And they will judge me.

Until then though, I am King. And I will reign as I see fit – with a double-barrelled iron rod, upon a tyrant throne of skin and bones.

08.07:
Magnolia:

Every morning I wake up and the first thing I see is a beige ceiling. I look around at my beige bedroom with its beige walls, and pull back my beige eiderdown. I tread softly on a beige shag pile, I draw the beige curtains and look out at the beige neighbourhood. Beige paperboys, white picket fences, and pristine lawns with beige begonias. Sprinklers water the yards, and beige people come out in beige gowns and beige slippers to say hello in beige tones.

Hello.

I go down to my beige kitchen and my beige wife has poured me a tall glass of orange juice and muesli with extra raisins.

Good for your digestion.

And I give my widest, beige-est smile, look at my beige children and the beige wall clock and the beige tiles and I just want to burn it all to the ground and fucking scream.

08.08:
Moonlight:

I had that same vision again last night.
In my dream, I went walking;
In the dead of night, I went walking,
And found myself at the forest edge.
Stepping into the trees,
I felt brambles wrap around me;

I finally look down at myself.
I look down at my self, at my body.
At my nakedness.
And I am glowing.
I am resplendent.
The moon beats down on me until I am a beacon.
My skin is translucent,
My fingers are white candle flames,
And my arms are wax rivers.

And I am dancing now.
I can no longer determine whether
I am man or woman,
Neither, both or all,
I can only see thick, thatched stains of pubic hair
Dark fairy rings of areolae.
Against stark whiteness.

In this open place.
In this copse.
In this thicket of thorns
I am a corpse,
Dancing on hidden strings.

08.09:
Old Lace:

I told my husband I found it by accident. That I uncovered it, like a grown teenager rereading school reports from his nursery years. Like a foolish man looks backs on photographs of when he used to be happy with someone else.

Of course, I knew it was there.

It rotted away in the background, festering at the back of my skull like a brutal injury, and no matter how many bandages I wrapped it in, no matter how tightly I tried to suppress it… Blood still seeped through to the surface.

And so I opened the box. I brushed off the years of dust and took it down from the attic and let it settle on the kitchen counter.

The box with the blanket in. The rattle. And the embroidered bonnet and booties. Each a harsh reminder; a suture in a tragic wound that never quite closed.

They'll say I was tired.
This is a precious lie. I was only forty-two, not the image of the old woman most people conjure up at the sound of my name.
I was no tired than I would normally be after the long working day, and I had slept soundly.
Tired is a misleading word, but it's true. I *was* tired. I was exhausted. I was ashamed, and sick of giving in.

I was sick of moving further down the bus.
I was tired of drinking at different water fountains.
I was pissed at being shot in the streets.
I was furious at being crushed underfoot and ground into sand.

No.

These sands are shifting.
We are beginning to fight for our rights. Our human freedoms. Our citizenship.
And one day, after these hardships and pressures, and heat…

…we will eventually become pearls.

Mama says I'm special.
She tells everyone – the neighbours, over garden fences. The other secretaries down at the bank. Old friends she meets in the canned goods aisles.

She's such a gifted child.
The talent just shines out of her.
She'll be rich and famous one day – you'll see. Her name will be up in
Hollywood lights.
They'll tell such stories about her.

But the truth of the matter is, I never enjoyed the theatre. I hated to be the centre of attention. I hated being pretty, and I despised my flawless complexion.
I crafted an image for myself. I wore my hair in pin-curls, and blood-red lipstick. I pranced around in corsets and suspender belts whilst cameras flashed; but I always looked pale and withdrawn.

Saddened by my own beauty, as one photographer once said.

If Mama could see me now, what would she think?
Would she be proud?

Honey?
Hon. – are you awake? …Listen. I've been thinking.

We've been together for quite some time now, and I've never even looked at another man, or been dissatisfied in *le boudoir*; but I just have to ask…

—No. Not even Fit Charlie with the big muscles. He practically lives in that gym – I doubt I'd even get my arms around his neck, let alone his—

—Stop interrupting me, Harold! I'm trying to be open here. With my feelings. You know, like the therapist told us—

…Yes. Yes, Fit Charlie is attractive. And yes, there was a time when Alan and James' offer of a threesome would have been most appealing; but that's beside the point…

—Listen, Hon. I just want to know – are we getting a little… …pedestrian? I mean, you haven't fisted me in ages, and I can't remember the last time I had you up in the sling…

09. GREY:

09.01:
Ash:

David has never really been appreciative of my line of work, and we both knew it. Whenever I try to talk about it, he simply shrugs and tells me that time repeats itself, and that we're doomed to recreate the mistakes of our ancestors.

Since I started the Italian dig, we've not spoken at all. No emails, no international phone calls. Not even a quick video chat over Skype. He pretends my trips don't exist.

Vesuvius exploded in pyroclastic flows and tidal-waves of mud, and buried Pompeii and Herculaneum underneath ash and rubble and earth.

I uncover a human form, and it takes nearly three days to figure out it is a woman. By the end of the week, I realise her fossilized form is shielding something.

A child.

My belly kicks, and there's a sudden spasm of pain. I clutch my abdomen tightly, and reach for the phone.

09.02:
Battleship Grey:

The first salvo scattered into the ocean and showered us with spray. I flinched, and looked across the bow.

Incoming!

Another salvo. Where were these missiles coming from? And why? More spray. Waves, higher than the steel chimneys, threatened to sweep the decks clear like a chess board. All of the pawns left floundering helplessly. The knights and the bishops washed overboard.

Direct hit!

Screaming. Panic. Dread. This ship was going down. We had failed in our mission. We were—

—Jimmy? Aren't you done yet? You've been in there for nearly an hour – you'll prune something rotten!

Jimmy sits up in the bath. Petulantly spitting out a mouthful of dirty water, he lets go of the plastic warship and it floats harmlessly to the surface. The bubbles have long since dissipated and the water just looks murky now.

I used to dream, towards the end. When you grew weak and frail and looked more like a haunted doll, and less like yourself.

You used to ask me what I dreamt about, and I'd make up fantastical stories, of how we'd slay dragons and demons together, running wild and powerful.

But in reality, I used to dream of our house. It was on fire, and I was in the house while the house burned down. I sat on a flaming armchair, and you'd enter, hair a glowing halo. You'd pin me down, fellate me, and leave sooty smears and fingerstains on my chest.

After you died, I walk in supermarkets. And under my clothes I feel burning hand-prints. I remember the heat and the glow and the fire.

After you died, I walk in supermarkets, and I stare at food labels. I do a lot of things.

They say it's darkest before the dawn.
And today's landscape is a photograph where no star shines.
I can see trees, but I cannot see forests.
I can hear waves, but I cannot find the ocean.
The lie of the land.

I listen at night.
I wait until that moment where the colours of the dark
Are the same regardless of whether my eyes are open or closed.
I wait until I cannot tell whether my eyes are open or closed.
I fool myself.

I wait for answers.
Questions smother me like sheets, and I wait for answers.
But in a world where the blind lead the blind;
And we feel our way,
I cannot help but cut off my own hands
Just to spite myself.

Next we have a special treat for you!

One hundred lucky viewers will be able to purchase a limited edition choker, made from rose quartz beads, refined haematite, the very rare cubic zirconia, and exquisitely hand-finished elements carved from the finest stainless steel!

See how it delicately catches the light – modelled here by the lovely Gloria – without appearing too gaudy or pretentious.

Haematite has long been known to encourage the blood supply, modern medicines' first defence against jaundice, anaemia, and leukaemia! Cubic zirconia is also a hidden weapon against most cancers of the skin and liver, so you too can enjoy an extra hour in the sunbed, sipping the finest champagne, and all the while looking simply fabulous.

For the stupendous bargain of only nineteen hundred and fifty pounds, you too could own this truly marvellous item. And for the first fifty buyers, we'll even throw in a matching bracelet!

Red.
A woman stands in the middle of the highway; wearing a rigid mask of disbelief. She looks at her hands as if she cannot comprehend what they are.

Blue.
Two men slow dance by the side of the road. One of them is crying. The other keeps his eyes fixed on the middle distance.

Red.
The reporter adjusts her earpiece, brushes her skirt down, and absently picks a piece of lint from her microphone.

Blue.
A fireman has to physically restrain a young woman after she starts screaming and clawing at the wreckage. He is struck across the cheek, but does not seem to mind.

Red.
The paramedic has only been on shift for twenty minutes. He is stunned. And simply watches.

Blue.
A hand twitches spasmodically from a metal coffin.

And the sirens flash in snapshots red and blue.

Pick a card, any card.
Flip a coin. Heads or tails?
Jack of Diamonds, Queen of Spades, King of Clubs,
Ace of Hearts. Royal flush. Lucky streak.
Sleight of hand. Game of chance.

Now, shuffle.

Flip a coin – where will it land?
Is this your card? Watch again.
This might only be a stream of consciousness.
Where will it go?
Round and round and round he goes.
Where he stops, nobody knows.
Roulette. Ante up.
Marked deck. Weighted dice. Dealer's choice.
Court cards with only one eye open.
Jack of Diamonds, King of Clubs, Joker.
Come to daddy. Younger seeks older.
Masc4masc. No Queens allowed.

Cut the deck.

Do you know your status?
I don't care, just put it in. Spit on it.
Gamble. The house always wins.
Ace of Hearts.
Practice taking topless selfies with your stomach held in.
Practice your Poker Face.
Don't forget to smile.

09.08:
Payne's Grey:

My art teacher taught me never to mix black paint into another colour. If you needed a darker shade, you didn't want the pigment to grow dull or dirty looking; so rather than use black, you simply added a bead of blue, or brown, or purple. Something to give a little vibrancy, and still change the tone.

I've begun to look at life in the same way. Sometimes we don't need to try so desperately. We don't need to simply go harder, or faster, or darker. Sometimes we just need a different perspective, and to add a little something new.

My art teacher was a very wise man. But for the life of me, I can't even remember his name.

Platinum:

Who is King of the castle?

Who decided the pecking order?

Who told us that sports should be the top of the pyramid, and that the trickle-down effect would run through all of the sciences, before the arts?

Who looked up one day and decided that stories, and poems, and paintings and plays and performances were worth nothing? That art and literature was expendable, and unnecessary?

Who stripped our curriculums?

Who sneered at a diploma in drama?

Who set flame to the canvas and threw our books on the fire?

Who wrote down on clipboards that imaginative children were just easily distracted?

Who ordered the nanny state?

Who indoctrinated the masses?

Who rallied the artists?

Who is simply watching the clock until we seize the throne?

Who would have thought that a little badge could cause so much trouble?

If it wasn't enough to win a medal, in a packed stadium with thousands of eyes on us, thousands of eyes glued to television sets…

The pressure was intense. He had forgotten his gloves, so I suggested they split the one pair they had between them. One each. A stand of solidarity.

America was rotten; and she couldn't smell the stench on her skirts. Couldn't see who the flames of liberty did and did not burn for.

The anthem began, and they bowed their heads behind me, and raised their fists. First came Martin Luther. Then Vietnam. This might only be the next step, but there was electricity. A storm in the air.

This is the house that Jack built.

This is the lounge, with beautiful leather finishes. All lovingly picked out by Jill. She has expensive taste. No leatherette here. Only the real thing.

In the den, Jack collects mounted heads and marble furniture and sharp edges. Jack is a masculine fine figure of a man. Jack wants everyone, including Jill, to know this. To know how much of a strong, breadwinning man Jack is. Money is no object.

Jill has padded out the kitchen with gadgets that Jack does not recognise. What even is a garlic press? When would one need to slice eggs? How many settings does one coffee-maker require?

Jill loves her life. She loves the home that Jack built. The home that Jack paid for. Jill smiles in the morning, and she smiles before she sleeps. Jill believes she is happy.

Jack is miserable and slowly going bankrupt.

09.12:
Smoke:

Mark the date.

Stop the clocks.

From now on, I am a fatherless son.
I can count on two still hands
All the things I never said and wished I had.
All the achievements I never earned in time.
But that is a fact that cannot change.

And never will.

Instead,
I'll lose my shit in Starbucks.
Because I can't get the paper sleeve to open properly.
And I'll buy more tobacco than I need
And look at the death rattle stickers.
And I'll try and focus on crossword puzzles I don't want to do,
But desperately cling to.

My mistake was thinking
I'd have to give them permission
To turn off the Machine.

It never even crossed my mind
That he might fail before I got there.

Mark the date.
23.12.2016
Stop the clocks.
19:22

10. BLACK:

I'm not scared.
I don't panic, or scream or do much of anything really.
I am simply alone with my thoughts; drifting among the stars.
The gauges are running low. Clocks and dials winding down.
Time is running out, and I don't mind.

The shuttle is gone. The crew are dead. It's just me now.
My helmet is an echo chamber of my own thoughts. The
sound of my breath is calming.
I float.
I float on a sea of stars and space.
For the last few minutes I am made of precious stars.

Spiralling into the void.
I just watch the little numbers count down and feel so
insignificant. I am just data.
And like an old soul, I remember the lives I have lived. I
imagine the sliding doors; the different choices I could have
made. And whether I'd be happier.

I'm not scared.
I am light. I am made of stars.

I am made of stars.
I am made of dust.
And I quietly go out without a fuss.

Calmly.
Fade
To

Black.